A BATPIG BOOK

WHEN PIGS FLY

ROB HARRELL

DIAL BOOKS FOR YOUNG READERS

DIAL BOOKS FOR YOUNG READERS
An imprint of Penguin Random House LLC, New York

First published in the United States of America by Dial Books for Young Readers, an imprint of Penguin Random House LLC, 2021

Visit us online at penguinrandomhouse.com.

Library of Congress Cataloging-in-Publication Data is available

Printed in China

ISBN 9780593354155 • 10 9 8 7 6 5 4 3 2 1
TOPL

Design by Jason Henry

For all the kids out there writing stories and drawing whenever you can: Keep going! I mean, look at this—it's a whole book about a pig in a cape. If I can do it, you can too!

STARTING NOW!
BATPIG
IN
SPACE FARCE
HOUSTON! WE HAVE AN ORIGIN STORY!
STORY #1
ACTION! SUSPENSE! SNACKS!

CHAPTER ONE

"LET'S DO THIS"

BATPIG WAS IN SERIOUS TROUBLE.
In some serious DOO-DOO, AREN'T YOU, MR. BATPIG?
SIGH
SSSSS
HE WAS STRAPPED TO A GIANT ROCKET BY THE POTTY-MOUTH REPTO-MAN. AND THE FUSE WAS LIT!

ON THE ROOF OF A TALL BUILDING, THE ROCKET WAS AIMED RIGHT AT THE SUN.
This is so pooping awesome!
SSS

AND HE'D SWALLOWED A POISON PILL, SO HE ONLY HAD MOMENTS TO DO SOMETHING!
THE SITUATION ISN'T IDEAL.
SSS

SUDDENLY, THE FUSE RAN OUT AND POOR BATPIG BLASTED OFF. REPTO-MAN YELLED SOMETHING POTTY-RELATED IN HIS EXCITEMENT.
OH, DEAR.
TOILET BRUSH!!
YESSS!

AS THE ROCKET CLIMBED, BATPIG PLANNED...
FIRST, I NEED TO BARF UP THIS POISON PILL!

HE HAD TO THINK OF SOMETHING GROSS ENOUGH TO MAKE HIM HURL.
MUSTARD AND OLIVE ICE CREAM!
MRS. HAWLEY'S TOENAIL COLLECTION!
WORM SPIT!

Worm spit did the trick.

AS THE POISON LEFT HIS SYSTEM, SOME TOUGH QUESTIONS CAME TO BATPIG.

WHERE DID I GO WRONG?

How did I end up here?

How can anybody like asparagus?

THEN HE FELT SOMETHING COMING. SOMETHING HAPPENING...

CHAPTER TWO

"STRANGE BEGINNINGS"

FLASHBACK ALERT!!

GARY YORKSHIRE WAS A PIG. A NORMAL, PINK, FUZZY, BORING OL' PIG...
Hey!

He LIVED WITH HIS PARENTS (IMA AND URA) IN A FOURTH-STORY WALK-UP IN BIG CITY, USA.
ARTSY PROFESSIONAL FAMILY PHOTO

He was a SIXTH GRADER AT BIG CITY MIDDLE SCHOOL, HOME OF THE FIGHTING BURRITOS.
WORST MASCOT EVER.

He liked what most pigs his age like: Tasty sandwiches...
Oh...oh OINK that's good.
PIG SODA
SLOP COOKIES

Video games...
SNORT SNORT SNORT
SNORT.

Reading comics...
HAHA! THE CRIMSON SWINE DOES IT AGAIN!

Mud baths...

Playing cards with friends...
We should make some sandwiches.

IT WAS A PRETTY NORMAL LIFE, THERE IN THE FANCY TERRACE APARTMENTS.

UNTIL ONE AFTERNOON...

GARY LOOKED OVER AND SAW THAT BROOKLYN HAD NODDED OFF.
Ha ha! Good ol' BROOK.
Z.

HE DECIDED TO TRY THAT THING WHERE YOU PUT SHAVING CREAM IN HER HAND AND TICKLE HER NOSE.
Bat Snore.
Hee Hee. This is Gonna Be SO GREAT!
SHE'S GONNA SMEAR IT ALL OVER HER...

BUT BROOKLYN WAS STARTLED AND BIT GARY RIGHT ON THE HONKER!
GAA!
YAAAA! MY HONKER!
CHOMP

OH NO!! I THOUGHT YOU WERE A MOSQUITO!
DO I LOOK LIKE A MOSQUITO??

BEFORE BROOKLYN LEFT, SHE PUT SOME OINTMENT ON GARY'S SNOUT.
Sorry again, buddy.
IT'S OKAY. It doesn't hurt that bad.
MAN! I go to the john for one minute and miss all the good stuff!

THAT NIGHT, GARY'S SNOUT THROBBED, AND HE DREAMED HE WAS A BIRD.
This is a weird dream.
That's a weird beak.

THE NEXT MORNING, GARY FELT WEIRD, SO HE CALLED BROOK.

I feel weird. You don't have rabies, do you?
YOO HOO

No, and that's an offensive thing to ask a bat.

SAYING HE WAS WAS DOING HOMEWORK, GARY LAY DOWN FOR A QUICK NAP, BUT SLEPT UNTIL IT WAS DARK OUT.

THEN HE WAS WIDE AWAKE ALL NIGHT!

THE NEXT DAY, HE ATE, LIKE, TEN TASTY SANDWICHES.
GOODNESS, GARY.
URP.

WHEN HE PUT ON HIS UNDERPANTS, HE ACCIDENTALLY GAVE HIMSELF A WEDGIE.
It's like I don't know my own strength!
And OW!

LATER, JUMPING ON HIS BED, HE JUST KIND OF... STAYED IN THE AIR. FLOATING!
ULP!
THIS isn't normal!

THEN, HE SAW RIGHT THROUGH THE WALL AND SAW MRS. HAWLEY'S GIANT COLLECTION OF CAT HAIRBALLS!
GROSS!
eh?
Meow.

AT LUNCH, HE TOLD BROOKLYN. (BUT NOT CARL. CARL WAS A GOOD FISH, BUT HE COULDN'T KEEP A SECRET AT ALL.)

I think I have... like... powers!

WHAT? Hey! STOP WHISPERING!

So that afternoon (while Carl was at his trombone lesson) Gary showed Brooklyn what was up.

HOW COULD this happen? IS it from you biting me?
Boy, I just don't...um...

Wait. You aren't RADioactive OR Something, Are you?
um...

maybe a little.

BROOK!! WHY DIDN'T you tell me?
IT never came up!

BUT GARY SOON SAW THE UPSIDE.

I'm like the CRIMSON SWINE!
It's both exciting AND terrifying!

GARY SPENT THE NIGHT READING OVER ALL OF HIS OLD CRIMSON SWINE COMIC BOOKS.

BUT GARY COULDN'T STOP THINKING ABOUT IT.

MISTER PIG-BAT?

OINK MAN?

PIG IN A CAPE?

THE PIGINATOR?

SUPERSWINE?

AND THEN... HE HAD IT.

CHAPTER THREE

"THEN AND NOW"

BUT, BACK to that ROCKET HEADED to the SUN. Remember that?

BATPIG WAS HOTTER THAN A HABANERO POPPER, WHAT WITH THE SUN BEING SO CLOSE AND ALL.

HE WAS THINKING HE WAS A GONER WHEN HE SAW SOMETHING COMING.

ASTEROIDS! COMIN' RIGHT AT HIM!!

IT WAS BAD.

TINK
OOF!
BONK
DANG!
OW!
SMACK!
OH, FOR THE...
OINK
EXCEPT...

One giant asteroid slammed into the tip of Batpig's rocket, knocking it off course.

SENDING HIM HURTLING TOWARD A DEADLY CRASH INTO THE EARTH.

BUT LET'S GET BACK TO OUR ORIGIN STORY, SHALL WE?

CAN YOU HELP
ME LEARN
TO FLY?
MEH.
SOUP

I MEAN, I CAN
FLOAT, SO WHY
NOT FLY TOO?
NAH.
SLURP

JUST ONE
LESSON?
I DON'T
KNOW...

WE'LL JUST
FLY AROUND
FOR A LITTLE
WHILE.
I'M
BUSY.

BROOKLYN, WHY
WON'T YOU-?
I'M AFRAID
OF HEIGHTS,
OKAY??

YOU SPILLED YOUR SOUP.
YES, I KNOW, GARY.

YOU COULD'VE JUST TOLD ME ABOUT THE HEIGHT THING, BROOK. WE'RE FRIENDS!
IT'S EMBARRASSING. I'M A FLYING MAMMAL, AFTER ALL.

So BROOKLYN agreed to train GARY... But from the GROUND.

meanwhile...
Hey, MRS. Pig! Is GARY around?

Hi, CARL. NO, I think He's off with BROOK somewhere.

Okay. Um... thanks.
sad eyes
trembling fish lips

CARL'S Pet LIZARD
JAWS
Sniff.
POTTY JOKE BOOK (LYING OPEN)
MAGIC Stuff

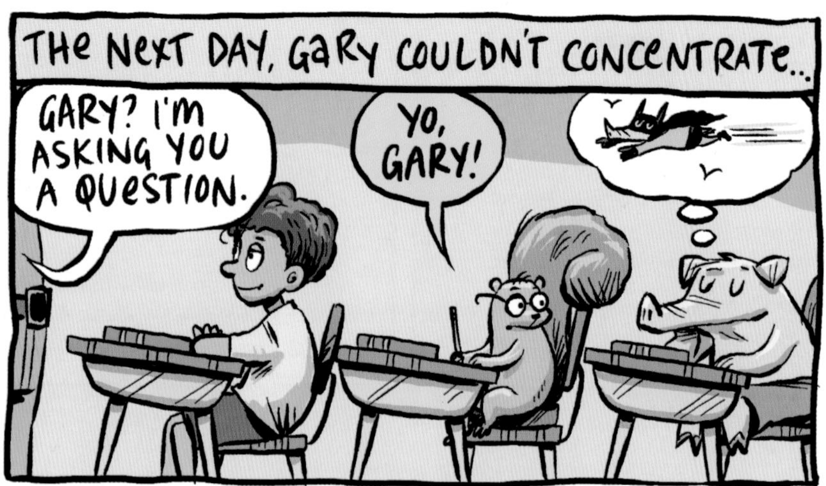
THE NEXT DAY, GARY COULDN'T CONCENTRATE...
GARY? I'M ASKING YOU A QUESTION.
YO, GARY!

HE HAD SO MANY THINGS TO TRY!
CAN I TOUCH A CLOUD?
CAN I SIT ON ONE?
WHAT DO CLOUDS TASTE LIKE?
I DON'T KNOW.
I DON'T KNOW.
I DON'T KNOW.

AND ALL THE BATPIG STUFF TO WORK OUT!
OH! I NEED A CATCHPHRASE, RIGHT?
WELL, OBVIOUSLY. TRY A FEW ON ME.

OINK IN THE NAME OF THE LAW!
MAKES NO SENSE.
THIS PIGGY'S GONNA MAKE YOU GO WEE WEE WEE ALL THE WAY HOME.
TOO LONG.
IF YOU'RE STEALIN', I'LL LEAVE YOU SQUEALIN'.
TOO SPECIFIC.
DOING CRIME DOESN'T BE-HOOVE YOU! GET IT?
I DON'T.
STOP OR I'LL PIG!!
THAT'S JUST DUMB.
LOOKS LIKE YOU'RE... HOG-TIED!
MAYBE YOU DON'T NEED A CATCHPHRASE.

BROOKLYN SHOWED GARY SOME COSTUME IDEAS SHE'D BEEN WORKING ON.
THIS ONE'S NEAT.
HOW WOULD I GO TO THE BATHROOM IN THAT?

THIS? SNAZZY, RIGHT?
WAIT. IS THAT SPANDEX?

I ENJOY THIS ONE.
TOO SWIRLY.

At Carl's place...

They wanna leave ME outta things?!

So, they don't like me anymore??

Traitors!! I thought we were friends!

Carl's kind of losing it.

WAAAAAAA

CHAPTER FOUR

"WHAT ABOUT CARL?"

ONE DAY AFTER SCHOOL, CARL DECIDED to FOLLOW BROOK + GARY. IN DISGUISE.
HUMMING A COOL, SNEAKY SPY SONG
CARL

AT the PARK, CARL HID IN SOME PLANTS AND WATCHED.
I SEE BROOK, BUT WHERE'S GARY?

UNTIL GARY FLEW DOWN OUT OF THE FLIPPIN' SKY!!
HOW'D THAT CLOUD TASTE?
LIKE DIRTY WATER. DO YOU HAVE A MINT?
GASP!!

WHAT the WHAT??
PIGS CAN'T FLY!!
AT LEAST I DON'T THINK SO.
I SHOULD PAY MORE ATTENTION TO THOSE THINGS.
SIRI, CAN PIGS FLY?
NO.
I KNEW IT!!

CARL WALKED HOME, CRUSHED.
THIS IS HUGE!! WHY WOULDN'T THEY HAVE TOLD ME??

COULD IT BE BECAUSE I'VE NEVER KEPT A SECRET LONGER THAN FOUR MINUTES??

NAH.
THEY'RE JUST BEING JERKS.

WHEN HE got home, HE GOT IN HIS BOWL, GRABBED HIS FISHPOD, AND PLAYED SOME OLD, SAD FISH SONGS.
I'M-a FEELIN' DOWN IN my gills...
SIGH.
NACHO CHEEZ FISH FLAKES

THAT NIGHT.
COME ON OUT. LET ME SEE IT!
WHATTAYA THINK?
OH, DANG!
BUT WILL IT STRIKE FEAR INTO THE HEART OF EVIL?
OH HECK YEAH, IT WILL!
GOOD. BUT IT'S A LITTLE TIGHT IN THE BOOTY REGION.
IT'LL STRETCH.
TAKE IT FOR A SPIN!

SO GARY... ER... BATPIG DID. HE SET OFF INTO THE NIGHT!

BATPIG! YONDER! HO!

(HE WAS STILL WORKING ON THE CATCHPHRASE.)

It was a busy night! Batpig stopped one woman from littering...

That Twix wrapper goes in the trash receptacle.

Okay, weirdo.

Um... that's a pig.

BUT ALSO, WEARING the SUIT MADE GARY FEEL CONFIDENT.
REALLY CONFIDENT.
MAN, I'M AWESOME.
OH, BROTHER.

FLYING BACK TO BROOKLYN'S HOUSE, GARY NOTICED A LIGHT ON IN CARL'S BEDROOM.

GOOD OL' CARL.
LET'S SEE WHAT HE'S UP TO.

AND WHAT HE SAW IN CARL'S WINDOW MADE HIM FEEL AWFUL.

LONELY SONG, LONELY SONG...

HE FLEW BACK IN A RUSH.

OH, AND IN THE PRESENT, BATPIG IS STILL SPEEDING TOWARD CERTAIN DOOM, YADDA YADDA YADDA...
OH, BY ALL MEANS, TAKE YOUR SWEET TIME WITH THE BACKSTORY.
I CAN WAIT.

CHAPTER FIVE

"PARTY TIME"

We've Been so BUSY. I HadN'T THOUGHT MUCH ABOUT CARL.
OOH, RIGHT.

I THINK He THINKS We DON'T LIKE HIM ANYMORe.
ReALLY? OH, THAT STINKS.

We SHOULD THROW A "CARL PARTY"!
WOW! IT'S LIKe THe SUIT MAKeS YOU SMARTeR TOO!

SO THEY STARTED PLANNING THE PARTY.
BALLOONS?
CARL DOES ENJOY A GOOD BALLOON.

THEY EVEN SENT CARL AN INVITATION (ON FANCY PAPER).
WOW!
YOU'RE INVIT

I BET THEY'LL TELL ME ALL ABOUT THE FLYING AND STUFF AT THE PARTY.
HA.
I'M SO SILLY.
SNIFF.
THEY PROBABLY PLANNED TO TELL ME LIKE THIS ALL ALONG.

HE SHOWED UP AT GARY'S, READY FOR AN EXPLANATION AND SOME FUN!

THE OLD GANG, BACK TOGETHER AGAIN!

DING DONG

HE EVEN BROUGHT COOKIES AND A COUPLE OF HIS NEW MAGIC TRICKS.

IT WAS A GREAT PARTY, CONSIDERING IT WAS JUST THE THREE OF THEM.
HAA!
YOU SMASHED ME! I'VE BEEN MUSHED!
THEY PLAYED VIDEO GAMES.

SO TASTY!
BEYOND TASTY!
THEY ATE TASTY SANDWICHES.
MMPH!

BUT FINALLY, CARL ASKED HIS BIG QUESTION.
SO... WHAT HAVE YOU GUYS BEEN SO BUSY WITH?

GARY AND BROOK FROZE.

CALISTHENICS!
TUMBLING!

CARL COULDN'T BELIEVE IT. THEY WERE LYING! FIBBING, RIGHT TO HIS FACE!
YOU'VE... BEEN BUSY TUMBLING AND DOING CALISTHENICS?

YEP! SOMERSAULTS! JUMPING JACKS!

WE'RE WORKING ON A ROUTINE!

SHOW ME.

SO, THEY DID. BADLY. THEY JUMPED AND ROLLED AROUND ON THE FLOOR, MAKING IT UP AS THEY WENT.
THEN I CARTWHEEL LIKE THIS!
AND I... UM... ROLL OVER THREE TIMES.

TA-DA!
PANT
PANT
SWEAT
THAT'S GREAT.
I'M GONNA GO.
YOU DON'T WANT TO FINISH YOUR TASTY SANDWICH?
I LOST MY APPETITE.
AS CARL LEFT THE APARTMENT BUILDING, HE NOTICED SOME WADDED PAPER IN A TRASH CAN.
WHAT'S THIS?
HE SAW BROOK'S HANDWRITING, SO HE GRABBED THE PAPER.

"BAtpig"
• STRONG
• FLY
Moves
IT WAS SOME OF THEIR SUPERHERO NOTES.

GARY'S A SUPERHERO??

They DIDN'T TELL ME?

WE'RE SUPPOSED TO BE FRIENDS!!

WHAT AM I? CHOPPED tUNA??

AND SOMETHING SNAPPED IN CARL.

CHOPPED TUNA. HA HA.
HA HA HA HA! HAH!!

Hee Hee
HAA HAAAA

WELL, IF THIS "BATPIG" IS A SUPERHERO, HE'S GOING TO NEED...
...A SUPER-VILLAIN!

MUAH HA HA HA!

CHAPTER SIX

"A HERO IN ACTION"

THAT NIGHT, BATPIG TOOK TO THE SKIES.
PROWLING FOR TROUBLE, OUR CAPED HERO...
HELP!!

WHAT'S THAT? AN ACTUAL CRY FOR HELP?
WITHOUT HESITATION, BATPIG FLEW TO THE RESCUE!

WHAT IF THERE'S, LIKE, REAL BAD GUYS?
OKAY, THERE WAS SOME HESITATION.

IGNORING HIS FEAR, HE FLEW INTO AN ALLEY WHERE A MUGGING WAS GOING DOWN.
STOP, THUG! I HEARD A SMALL GOAT CRY FOR HELP!
?
I...I MEAN... I YELLED. BUT I'M A MAN.
YOU DO HAVE KIND OF A BABY GOAT VOICE.
OH, SO I'M GETTING MUGGED AND MADE FUN OF? THAT'S JUST GREAT.
TRY PROJECTING FROM YOUR DIAPHRAGM MORE.
UNIMPORTANT! THIS ROBBERY IS OVER!!

THE ROBBER PERSISTED.
OH, NOT REALLY. WE WERE JUST GETTING STARTED.
NONSENSE!! BATPIG IS HERE!
RIIIIIGHT. AND WHAT'S A BATPIG?
ALLOW ME TO SHOW YOU.

Batpig used his moving-stuff-with his-brain power to disarm and confuse the criminal.

What the...?

I've lost my bad guy weapon!

And gravity!

Whoa.

Fear not! I'll take this hoodlum to the police!

Thank you, Batpig!
Except for the voice thing. That was awkward.

BATPIG FLOATED THE BADDIE STRAIGHT TO THE AUTHORITIES.
WHY THE STRIPED ROBBER SHIRT? IT GIVES YOU AWAY.
RIGHT? I JUST SPACED!

AND THE POLICE COULDN'T HAVE BEEN MORE EXCITED.

THERE'S A MASKED PIG LEVITATING A BAD GUY OUT FRONT.

SHH. THE CRIMSON SWINE IS ON.

OINK!

BUT THE LEGEND OF BATPIG WAS BORN THAT NIGHT.
YEP. A LITTLE PIG. HAD A SUIT AND EVERYTHING.

IT EVEN MADE THE PAPERS!

BIG CITY TIMES

MCRIB IS BACK

BELOVED SANDWICH RETURNS

PIG IN MASK STOPS

CHAPTER SEVEN

"THINGS GET WEIRD"

MEANWHILE, CARL WAS WORKING ON SUPERVILLAIN STUFF.
LET'S SEE. WHAT KIND OF EVIL DOES "THE FISHMONGER" GET UP TO?

OH, YEAH. HE'S CALLING HIMSELF "THE FISHMONGER" NOW.

I COULD JUMP OUT AND YELL BOO!

SHORT SHEET HIS BED!

REACH BEHIND HIS BACK AND TAP HIS SHOULDER SO HE'S ALL LIKE WHAAAAAA??

THEN CARL HAD "THE IDEA."
OH! I'LL PUT NACHO CHEEZ FISH FOOD IN A PIG SODA!

THEN ILL HAVE HIM OVER AND OFFER IT TO HIM...

AND HE'LL TAKE A SIP...

AND IT'LL BE ALL GROSS!
HA HA MUAH!

IT WAS PERFECT.

Hey, Gary. Wanna come play video games?

Sure!

WITH GARY ON HIS WAY, CARL WHIPPED UP HIS HORRIBLE CREATION.
DANG, THAT SMELLS AWFUL.
LIKE BURPS AND FEET.

BUT LITTLE DID CARL KNOW, THE COMBO CAUSED A CHEMICAL REACTION!
SSSSS
POP
FIZZ
PIG SOD
AN AWFUL REACTION.

WHEN GARY ARRIVED, CARL MADE HIS SINISTER OFFER.
GARY, WOULD YOU LIKE A DELICIOUS PIG SODA?
PIG SODA

NAH, I'M GOOD.

BUT YOU LOVE PIG SODA.

I JUST HAD ONE. PUT IT ON THAT SHELF FOR LATER!
THE SHELF ABOVE YOUR LIZARD!

AN ANGRY CARL PLACED THE SODA ON THE SHELF ABOVE HIS LIZARD.

AND HE SLAMMED HIS BEDROOM DOOR AS HE LEFT, TIPPING THE SODA.

PIG SOD

SSSS

PIG SODA

WINK

SSSSS

OH, DEAR.

CARL AND GARY WERE HAVING SUCH A GREAT TIME, CARL FORGOT ALL ABOUT THE SODA!
HEY! YOU CAN'T MUSH MY SMASHER AFTER A POWER-UP!
NO! I GOT RESMASH-INATED, REMEMBER?

THEN GARY HAD TO GO HOME, AND CARL FELT PRETTY GOOD ABOUT THINGS.
I FEEL SWELL!
THAT VILLAIN STUFF WAS DUMB ANYWAY.

BUT... WHAT HE FOUND IN HIS ROOM LEFT HIM STUNNED.
GASP!

THIS is POOPIN' AWESOME!

WHA...? WHO??
IT'S ME, REPTO! YOUR PET LIZARD! I GOT SUPER BIG!

HOW? AND HOW CAN YOU TALK?

I GUESS IT WAS THE PIG SODA MIXTURE!
IT'S LIKE A POTION!

AND WHY ARE YOU WEARING MY BOW TIE AND MAGICIAN HAT?
UH... BECAUSE I LOVE MAGIC! DUH!

BUT NOW I CAN HELP YOU DESTROY BATPIG! TWO SUPERVILLAINS WORKING TOGETHER!

"DESTROY" SEEMS LIKE A HARSH WORD.

WHAT?? AFTER HE LEFT YOU OUT? HIM AND THAT BAT?

LISTEN. I THINK I JUMPED THE GUN A LITTLE. GARY'S A GOOD GUY. AND BROOK'S AWESOME. I DON'T THINK THEY MEANT TO–

I'M REPTO-MAN NOW. 'CAUSE IT SOUNDS SO POOPIN' COOL.

BUT WHAT TO DO ABOUT YOU? THAT PIG HAS OBVIOUSLY BRAINWASHED YOU. YOU'RE ALL... WISHY-WASHY.

MINUTES LATER, CARL WAS TAPED TO HIS HEADBOARD. THERE WAS A HUGE HOLE IN HIS WALL, AND A GIANT LIZARD WAS ON THE LOOSE.
BATPIG MUST DIE!
Mmmph!!
NOT THE BEST OF DAYS.

CHAPTER EIGHT

"LIZARDS AND ROCKETS AND STREET SIGNS. OH MY!"

ABOUT THAT TIME, GARY WAS TELLING BROOKLYN ABOUT "BATPIG'S BIG NIGHT."
SO, YOU AND THE ROBBER FOUGHT?
ARE THERE MORE SAND-WICHES?
NO.
DANG.
BUT, YEAH! WE HAD A HUGE BATTLE.
MM-HMM. SO, WHY DON'T YOU HAVE ANY BRUISES?
I MUST HAVE SUPER HEALING OR SOMETHIN'!

JUST THEN, A REPORT CAME ON THE TV.
A GIANT LIZARD MAGICIAN IS SMASHING STUFF AND TELLING FART JOKES DOWNTOWN.
IT'S A GAS, GET IT??
IF ONLY WE HAD SOME SORT OF CAPED HERO WHO COULD SAVE THE DAY!!
I THINK THAT'S FOR YOU.
YEAH, BUT... HOOO BOY! I WASN'T EXPECTING A GIANT MAGIC LIZARD RIGHT OFF THE BAT!

I'LL GET YOUR BATPIG SUIT.

OKAY. OR CALL THE ARMY OR...

SCREAM!
BOOM

BUT ONCE IN HIS SUIT THE "BATPIG CONFIDENCE" SET IN, AND GARY WAS READY FOR ACTION.

ONE FRIED LIZARD, COMIN' UP.

DOWNTOWN, HE FOUND REPTO-MAN IN ALL OF HIS CAR-SMASHING, POTTY-JOKE-TELLING GLORY...

HAVE I TOLD THE ONE ABOUT THE SMELLY TOILET?

NOT AGAIN!

AAAA

FIRST, THE NAME IS REPTO-MAN.

THIRD, I SEE MY PLAN TO LURE YOU OUT INTO THE OPEN WORKED...

THIRD... WAIT. I ALREADY SAID THIRD. DID I SKIP SECOND?
DANG IT, REPTO, YA DIAPER HEAD.

SO THAT I CAN DESTROY YOU, PIGBAT!!

IT'S "BATPIG".

OH, SORRY. WHAT'D I SAY?

WITH THAT, BATPIG ATTEMPTED TO MIND-LIFT REPTO-MAN INTO THE AIR.

HNNGGHH!
WHAT ARE YOU DOING? THAT TICKLES!

BUT THE SLITHERY FIEND WAS TOO HEAVY!

SO HE SWEPT IN AND STOLE HIS HAT.
HA!
WHAT THE..?

WHY THE HAT? NOT COOL!!
IT ONLY MADE REPTO-MAN ANGRIER.

INSTEAD, HE GRABBED REPTO'S TAIL.

GOTCHA!

AND THREW HIM AS HARD AND AS FAR AS HE COULD...

LOUD SLAM!

AW, POOP!

SIG

ACCIDENTALLY SMASHING INTO A STREET SIGN IN THE PROCESS.

UNFORTUNATELY, REPTO-MAN SMASH-LANDED THROUGH THE ROOF OF A GIANT-SPACE-ROCKETS-R-US.

CRASHH!

GIANT-SPACE-ROCKETS-R-US

SALE!

(I THINK WE ALL SEE WHERE THIS IS HEADED.)

BACK AT CARL'S, HIS MOM FOUND HIM DUCT-TAPED TO THE BED.
MPH!
CARLY-POO? WHY ARE YOU TAPED TO THE BED? AND WHY IS THERE A GIANT-LIZARD-SIZED HOLE IN THE WALL?

SHE RELEASED HIM, PULLING OFF A FEW SCALES IN THE PROCESS.

NO TIME TO EXPLAIN, MOM! GARY AND BROOK ARE IN TROUBLE!

BE CAREFUL, CARLY-POO!

CARL TOOK OFF AT A SPRINT.

CHAPTER NINE

"CALM DOWN. ALMOST THERE."

REPTO-MAN CAME OUT OF THE GIANT-SPACE-ROCKETS-R-US, HIS ARMS FULL.

WELL, THAT WORKED OUT GREAT FOR MY EVIL PLANS!

SPACE ROCKET KIT

THEN HE NOTICED THE STORE NEXT DOOR.
US
SERIOUSLY? WHAT ARE THE ODDS?
POISON PILL MART
SPACE ROCKET KIT

BACK DOWNTOWN, HE FOUND THE UNCONSCIOUS BATPIG (AS WELL AS HIS MAGICIAN'S HAT).

HE WENT TO THE TOP OF THE CLOSEST BUILDING TO ASSEMBLE HIS ROCKET.

THEN HE WOKE BATPIG UP, FORCE-FED HIM A POISON PILL, SHOT HIM INTO SPACE, BLAH BLAH, BLAH, BLAH. WE GET IT!
OKAY. NOW WE'RE CAUGHT UP.

AS CARL RAN BY BROOKLYN'S HOUSE HE SPOTTED HER COMING OUT.
GARY'S IN TROUBLE! I MEAN BATPIG!
I KNOW! I SAW ON THE NEWS!

HOW... HOW DO YOU KNOW ABOUT BATPIG?

I KNOW EVERYTHING, OKAY? WE'LL TALK ABOUT IT LATER!

WAIT? REPTO? YOUR REPTO??

YES! HE'S GIANT AND EVIL NOW!

TRY TO KEEP UP!

WHAT CAN WE DO? GARY'S IN SPACE!

HE'S A SMART PIG. HE'LL FIGURE SOMETHING OUT.

MAYBE.

THEY FOUND REPTO AT THE HOT DOG HUT, EATING A CHILI DOG AND WATCHING THE SKIES.
DANG IT! HE'S COMING BACK THIS WAY!
HOW'D HE MANAGE THAT??
!
!

GARY'S ROCKET IS COMING BACK!!
I KNOW!
WE NEED TO STOP IT BEFORE IT CRASHES!
I KNOW!
CAN YOU FLY US UP AND I'LL CUT HIS RESTRAINTS BEFORE HE LANDS!
GULP
I'M AFRAID OF HEIGHTS.
WHAT? SERIOUSLY?

BUT... IT'S TO SAVE GARY'S LIFE.
I KNOW.
THAT'S WHY I'M GONNA TRY.
SWEET!! I BROUGHT GOGGLES JUST IN CASE!

CHAPTER TEN

"Back To Earth"

BATPIG ONLY HAD MAYBE A MINUTE UNTIL IMPACT. HE WASN'T FEELING POSITIVE.
I MAY HAVE PEED A LITTLE.

HE HAD HIS EYES CLOSED TIGHT WHEN HE THOUGHT HE HEARD HIS NAME.
GARY!

WAS HE LOSING IT?
H...HELLO?

WE CAME TO SAVE YOU!!
I'M FREAKING OUT!!

THEY LATCHED ONTO THE ROCKET AND CARL STARTED SAWING AWAY.
YOU GUYS CAME!
OF COURSE WE CAME, DUDE!
WE'RE GONNA DIE!

FINALLY, THE RESTRAINTS BROKE AWAY. JUST IN TIME.

BATPIG CARRIED BROOK AND CARL OUT OF HARM'S WAY AS THE ROCKET CRASHED.
BOOM
I'M OKAY. I'M OKAY. I'M OKAY.

BUT WHAT NOW?
NOW I NEED TO SAVE THE CITY. BUT HOW?
I HAVE AN IDEA.
OH! (KISS KISS) SWEET EARTH! (KISS) I'M NEVER LEAVING YOU AGAIN!

REPTO CHANGED AFTER I PUT NACHO CHEESE FLAKES IN YOUR SODA AND IT GOT ON HIM.
MAYBE IF YOU MIXED THE OPPOSITE OF NACHO CHEESE FLAKES, IT'LL CHANGE HIM BACK.
WAIT.
WHY DID YOU PUT FLAKES IN MY SODA?
NO TIME! CITY TO SAVE!!

SO... WHAT'S THE OPPOSITE OF NACHO CHEESE FISH FLAKES?
I DON'T KNOW. WHAT?
COOL RANCH FISH FLAKES!!
AH, YES. BUT WHERE WOULD I GET SOME AT THIS TIME OF–
I BROUGHT SOME. AND A PIG SODA TOO.

AND WITH THAT, THEY HAD A PLAN.

BATPIG TOOK THE NASTY INGREDIENTS AND FLEW OFF TO FIND REPTO-MAN.

YOU OKAY?

STILL MIGHT BARF. GIVE ME A MINUTE.

CHAPTER ELEVEN

"UNFINISHED BUSINESS"

BATPIG FOLLOWED THE TRAIL OF RUBBLE AND CHILI STRAIGHT TO REPTO-MAN.
WE MEET AGAIN, REPTO.
AAAAH, MISTER PIG. I'VE BEEN LOOKING FOR YOU.

MAYBE WE CAN HASH THIS OUT WHILE I'M AWAKE THIS TIME.

IT'S NOT MY FAULT YOU WERE SLEEPING ON THE JOB, SWINE.

NOW FLY OVER HERE SO I CAN END YOU!!

BUT BATPIG HAD COME PREPARED.

THAT SOUNDS GREAT, BUT FIRST I HAVE A POTTY-HUMOR JOKE FOR YOU.

OH! SERIOUSLY? I LOVE JOKES!

I HAVE A BOOK OF 'EM I READ ALL THE TIME!
CLAP
CLAP
CLAP
TELL ME! TELL ME!

REPTO-MAN WAS STUMPED. HE DIDN'T KNOW THIS ONE.

Because it GOT STUCK in a crack.

FOR a LONG MOMENT, THE HUGE LIZARD SAID NOTHING.

BUT THEN HE SMILED AND BEGAN TO LAUGH.
HEH.

AND LAUGH...
HA! A CRACK!

AND LAUGH.
HA! HA! HA!

THEN THE HORRIBLE FOE WAS CLUTCHING HIS SIDES...

OH, THAT'S GREAT. A BUTT CRACK!

AND ROLLING ON THE GROUND IN FITS OF LAUGHTER.

HAHAH

THAT'S WHEN BATPIG MADE HIS MOVE.

GET SMALL!!

SPRAY!

NO!!

FIZZ

SO ZESTY!!

IT TOOK A SECOND, BUT THEN REPTO-MAN BEGAN TO SHRINK.
AW, FER CRYIN' OUT LOUD!

MY...WORDS... NOT... SPEAK...

POOP!

...

HA!

BATPIG SWEPT IN AND GRABBED THE COOL-RANCH-SCENTED BADDIE.
EW. STICKY.

HE FLEW BACK TO CARL AND BROOKLYN.
BAD LIZARD!

AND THEN THE THREE TOOK OFF FOR CARL'S TO PLAY VIDEO GAMES.

AND MAYBE SOME TASTY SANDWICHES?
SIGH.
YES, GARY, WE CAN HAVE SANDWICHES.
THE END
NO! WAIT! NOT THE END!

WAIT A SECOND!!
WHY DID YOU GUYS KEEP THE WHOLE BATPIG THING FROM ME?

BECAUSE YOU CAN'T KEEP A SECRET.

YEP. THAT MAKES SENSE.

BUT YOU HAVE TO KEEP THIS SECRET, CARL.
SERIOUSLY.
BUT IT'S SO HAAARD!!
OKAY. THAT'S THE END.
OR THE BEGINNING??

INTERMISSION!!
BROOKLYN and CARL in
"SECRET, SECRET"
KEEP READING. BUB.
KEEPING SECRETS FOR DUMMIES
STORY #2

CARL AND BROOKLYN ARRIVED AT SCHOOL AS CARL FINISHED HIS WORM SMOOTHIE.
SHLUUURRPP! AHH!!!
BIG CITY MIDDLE SCHOOL
CARL'S MOM MADE THE BEST WORM SMOOTHIES ON THE PLANET.

GARY WAS WAITING (CONVENIENTLY) BY THE TRASH CAN BY THE FRONT DOOR.

GO BURRITOS!
WHAT'S UP, SUPER GARY?
CARL!! SHHH!

DO YOU THINK HE'S GOT IT?

I REALLY DON'T KNOW.

JANICE! LOVE THE BANGS!

MOMENTS LATER, JESSICA ANGELFISH, THE MOST POPULAR, COOL FISH IN SCHOOL (AND CARL'S CRUSH), WALKED UP TO HIM.
Hey, Carl.
SHE ACTUALLY SPOKE TO HIM!

Um...Hello, Jessica. How perfectly normal for you to know my name!

How was your weekend?

CARL'S WEEKEND WAS SPENT SAVING THE CITY WITH BROOK AND GARY/BATPIG!

Um...

WHAT SHOULD HE DO? JESSICA NEVER SPOKE TO HIM, AND NOW HE HAD AN AMAZING STORY TO IMPRESS HER!
IT'S A SECRET! YOU PROMISED!!
TELL HER!! TELL HER!!
CARL STARTED SWEATING. (FISH SWEAT: EXTRA GROSS)

ARE YOU OKAY? YOU LOOK CLAMMY.
Hey!
HA HA. MY WEEKEND WAS REALLY... SUPER.
OH, YEAH? HOW SO?
CARL COULD FEEL THE SECRET CRAWLING UP HIS THROAT. HIS FISH LIPS WERE STARTING TO FORM THE WORDS "GARY HAS SUPERPOWERS."
SECRET, RIGHT ON LIPS

OH, NO! HERE IT COMES!

HE DID IT!! CARL MADE SOMETHING UP TO PROTECT THE SECRET!!

DURING THIRD PERIOD, BROOKLYN FOUND CARL HYDRATING IN THE BATHROOM.

I THOUGHT I MIGHT FIND YOU IN HERE.

No GIRLS allowed IN THe BOYS' ROOM, BROOK.

I'M PROUD OF YOU, BUDDY.
FOR HUMILIATING MYSELF IN FRONT OF JESSICA?
OR FOR HIDING OUT IN A TOILET?
FOR KEEPING A SECRET. I KNOW IT WASN'T EASY.
YEAH.
IT WASN'T.

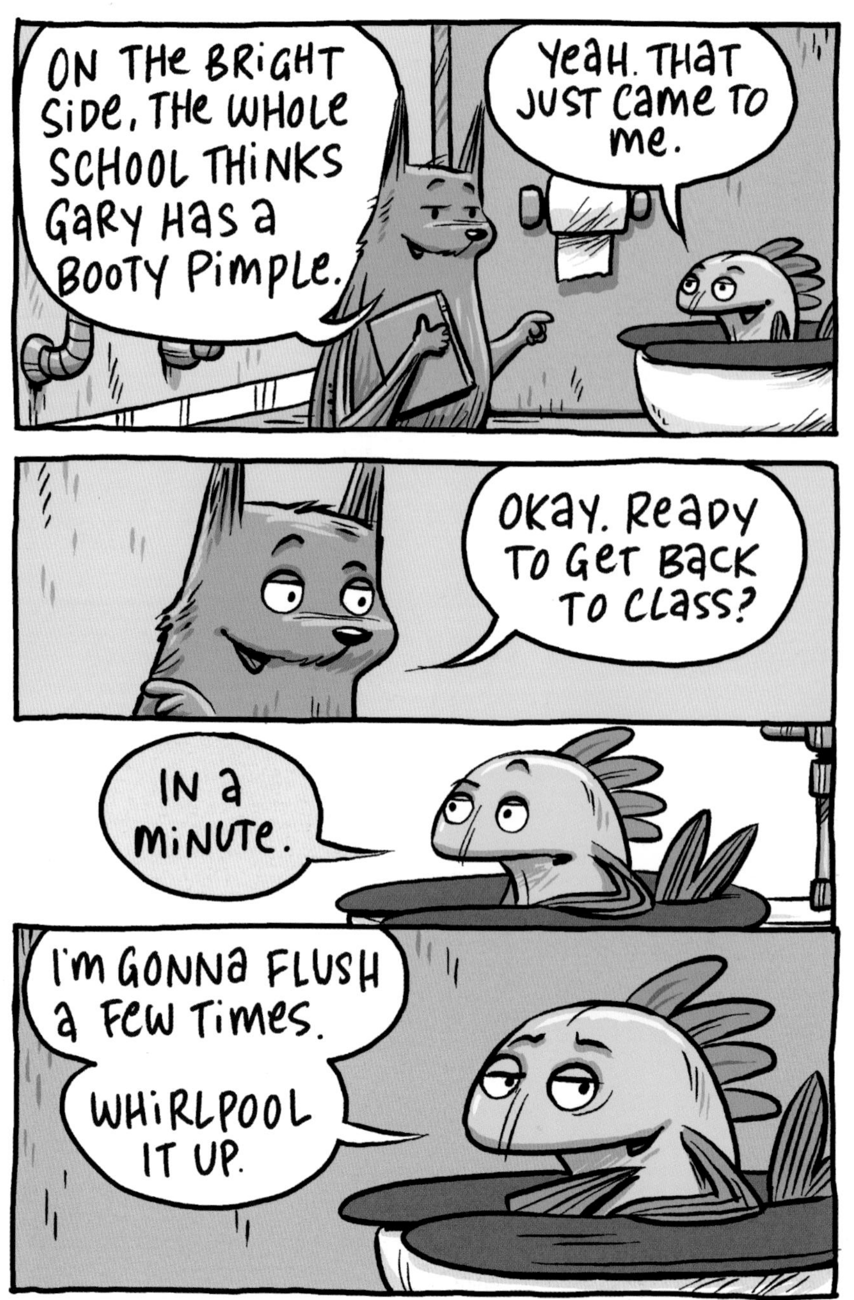
ON THE BRIGHT SIDE, THE WHOLE SCHOOL THINKS GARY HAS A BOOTY PIMPLE.
YEAH. THAT JUST CAME TO ME.
OKAY. READY TO GET BACK TO CLASS?
IN A MINUTE.
I'M GONNA FLUSH A FEW TIMES.
WHIRLPOOL IT UP.

BROOKLYN LEFT THE BOYS' ROOM A LITTLE MORE SURE CARL "GOT IT."
BOYS
GOOD OL' CARL. I THINK HE'S REALLY COMING ALONG.
FLUSH
FLUSH
THE END

UP NEXT!
BATPIG
IN
MEAT THE ENEMY
SIZZLE
ADVENTURE! A ROBOT! BREAKFAST FOOD!
STORY #3!

CHAPTER ONE

"A GOOD DAY RUINED"

OUR HERO, BATPIG, FOUND HIMSELF IN A HORRIBLE PREDICAMENT!
CURSES! WHY DOTH FATE HATE ME SO!!

HE HAD STEPPED IN SOME STICKY GUM.
GRUMBLE... HERO... NO RESPECT...
I MEAN, IT WAS SUPER STICKY.

LIKE, WALK-HOME-IN-ONE-BOOT STICKY.
I WILL AVENGE YOU, BOOT!

GARY (AKA BATPIG) FELL ASLEEP THINKING OF WAYS TO MAKE THE STREET SAFER.
NO-STICK SHOES?
GUM SCRAPERS ON EVERY CORNER?
NO-STICK SIDEWALKS?
OUTLAW GUM! NO GUM!
PACKS OF HUNGRY GUM-EATING POSSUMS?

THE NEXT MORNING—WATCHING HIS STEP—GARY SET OUT FROM HIS BUILDING HEADED FOR SCHOOL.
WOW! IT'S A BEAUTIFUL DAY IN THE NEIGHBORHOOD!

UNFORTUNATELY, HE HAD TO PASS THE STORE NEXT DOOR... "THE MEAT LADY."

OH, MAN.

DO I CROSS THE STREET TO AVOID HER TODAY?

MEAT LAD

OPEN

NO! I'M GONNA GO FOR IT.

BUT JUST AS HE STARTED, THE MEAT LADY OPENED THE DOOR TO MAKE HER TERRIBLE MEAT JOKES.
HEY, HEY, PORKCHOP!
WHAT'S SHAKIN', BACON?
LOOKIN' DELICIOUS TODAY!

HOW DID SHE ALWAYS KNOW WHEN GARY WAS ABOUT TO WALK BY?

IS IT A HAM-TASTIC DAY OR WHAT?

OINK OINK! HA HA!
IT WAS AWFUL.

HE TOLD BROOK AND CARL ABOUT IT AT LUNCH.
I DON'T KNOW IF SHE THINKS IT'S FUNNY OR IF SHE'S JUST...
A JERK?
AN EVIL JERK FACE?

WELL, FORGET ABOUT HER.

YEAH, WE'RE GONNA PLAY "SUPER MUSHERS 3" AT MY HOUSE TONIGHT.

OH! YOU GOT IT?? I HEARD IT'S MUSHIER THAN 2!

BUT THEN GARY REMEMBERED...
OH, NO. WAIT.

THE AWFULNESS OF WHAT HE HAD TO DO MADE HIS TAIL AND HOOVES GO ICE COLD.

I HAVE TO BABYSIT MY COUSIN TONIGHT.

YOU MEAN MERVIN??
WHAT THE WHAT?
M-MAYBE I CAN SAY I'M SICK!
OR FAKE MY DEATH!
OR FLEE THE COUNTRY?
WHY WOULD YOU AGREE TO THAT??
MY PARENTS MADE ME!!
OH, WOW. MERVIN IS THE WORST.

MERVIN WAS, IN FACT, THE WORST.
I'M MERVIN!

SUPER-SPOILED MERVIN AND HIS FAMILY LIVED DOWN THE HALL FROM GARY AND HIS FAMILY.
MERVIN'S PLACE
GARY'S PLACE

MERVIN'S TANTRUMS WERE FAMOUS IN THE NEIGHBORHOOD, AND HIS WHINING COULD BE HEARD FROM SPACE.

BUT MOMMY, I WANT A BLUUUUE ONE! A BLUE ONE! BLUE! BLUE! NOOOOOOOO!!

He was the pickiest eater that ever lived.

No, this peanut butter is too peanut-y and too butter-y!

He asked more questions than any kid alive.

Why?
What are questions?
Why is why spelled W-H-Y?

And maybe worst of all...

Superheroes are stupid! And dumb!!

BUT, GARY HAD AGREED, SO AT 6:30 HE WAS READY, WAITING FOR THE KNOCK AT THE DOOR.
I'M NOT READY. I'M SO NOT READY.
KNOCK KNOCK

GARY'S PARENTS LEFT WITH HIS AUNT AND UNCLE.
STAY OUT OF TROUBLE! HA HA!
HA.

AND THEN HE AND MERVIN WERE ALONE.
YOU'RE BORING.
WELL, YOU'RE AWFUL.

GARY TRIED TO COME UP WITH SOME ACTIVITIES.
WE COULD... DO A PUZZLE?
BORING!!
PIG SO

WE COULD...BUILD A COUCH FORT!
BORING-ER!!
PIG SO

I COULD LOCK YOU IN A CLOSET AND GO ABOUT MY EVENING?
NO NO NO! I WANT EXCITEMENT! I WANT ADVENTURE!!
PIG SO

CHAPTER TWO

STARTLING RiiiiiNGGGG!!

"ASK AND YE SHALL RECEIVE"

GARY'S PHONE RANG. IT WAS BROOKLYN.
GARY! TURN ON THE TV! SOMEONE BROKE INTO THE YUMMY YUMMY BISCUIT FACTORY!
GASP! BUT I LOVE YUMMY YUMMY BISCUITS!
THE CULPRIT HAS TAKEN OVER THE AIRWAVES. IT'S A SUPERVILLAIN!!
SHE CALLS HERSELF "THE BUTCHER"! THE CITY NEEDS BATPIG!!
BUTCHER

OH, REALLY? HUH. I DIDN'T HEAR THE SPECIAL RINGTONE.

SIGH. THIS AGAIN.

I KNOW, GARY. I'M SORRY I HAVEN'T CREATED A BATPIG RINGTONE FOR YOU YET.

I'M JUST SAYING... I'D FEEL SUPER NEEDED IF MY PHONE WENT "OINK OINK OINK" OVER SUPER COOL MUSIC.

YES! OKAY! WE'LL MAKE YOU ONE. BUT THE CITY NEEDS YOU NOW!

OKAY. GOOD. I'LL GO SAVE THE...
...
OH.
WHAT?
I CAN'T DO IT! I'VE GOT MERVIN!
IT'S FINE! CARL AND I'LL COME OVER TO WATCH MERVIN.
WHAT?

IT WAS SETTLED. BROOK AND CARL SHOWED UP JUST A BIT LATER.

HEY, MERVIN.

SO, MERV...

WHAT'S HAPPENING? WHY ARE A BAT AND A STINKY FISH HERE??

I'M TELLING!

WHILE GARY CHANGED, HE COULD HEAR MERVIN FLIPPING OUT IN THE OTHER ROOM.
AS THE BABYSAT, I HAVE RIGHTS!
I DEMAND PIZZA!
NO! TWO PIZZAS!

HE WAS PUTTING ON HIS BOOTS WHEN MERVIN BURST THROUGH THE BEDROOM DOOR.

WHOA. WHY ARE YOU WEARING A MASK AND UNDERPANTS?

!

SLAM

CRIM

SWINE

(LOOK AT CARL KEEPING A SECRET! GO CARL!)

BUT THEN HE WAS OFF TO FACE...
THE BUTCHER!!

WHICH IS WORSE? WATCHING MERVIN OR A SUPERVILLAIN?

IT WAS A TOSS-UP.

CHAPTER THREE

"SIZZLE, SIZZLE"

WHEN BATPIG REACHED THE FACTORY, HE SPOTTED THE BUTCHER, SITTING ATOP THE WORLD-FAMOUS YUMMY YUMMY BISCUIT SIGN ON THE ROOF.

OH, DEAR.
BIG CITY! I RULE THE BISCUITS!
YUMMY YUMMY

WHO COULD THIS MASKED VILLAIN BE??

THINK, BATPIG, THINK!

COME ON, NOGGIN!

AND WHY DID SHE HATE BISCUITS?

MEAT MY DEMANDS, OR THE FACTORY BURNS!

YUMMY

↑SEE THAT? SHE SAID "MEAT" INSTEAD OF "MEET" 'CAUSE SHE'S A BUTCHER. LOL!

THE HORRIBLE VILLAIN WENT ON TO EXPLAIN WHAT SHE WANTED.

I WANT TWO MILLION DOLLARS, A MID-SIZED MINI-VAN, SOME REESE'S PEANUT BUTTER CUPS...

YUMMY YUMMY

BISCUIT CO

...AND THE TRUE IDENTITY OF BATPIG!
EVIL LAUGH, EVIL LAUGH!

THE CROWD PANICKED.

NO!!

NOT MY FAVORITE BISCUITS!!

SERIOUSLY! HAVE YOU TRIED 'EM WITH BUTTER AND JELLY??

I HAVE! OH, I HAVE!!

BATPIG STRAINED HIS BRAIN TO FIGURE OUT WHO THE BUTCHER COULD BE.
LET'S SEE. A BUTCHER...
SHE'S A WOMAN...
DO I KNOW ANYONE LIKE THAT??
THE MEAT
SHE CARVES MEAT!
STRAIN STRAIN.
NOPE. I GOT NOTHING.
LOUSY BRAIN.

He HAD NO CHOICE BUT TO CONFRONT HER.
HERE GOES NOTHING.
FLY FLY
THE MEAT LADY

HELLO, BUTCHER.
JERK.

THE BUTCHER TURNED SLOWLY.
WELL, IF IT ISN'T THE HERO PIG.

TELL ME WHO YOU REALLY ARE, PIGLET.
B

IT WENT ON LIKE THIS FOR A WHILE.

FINALLY, BATPIG GOT TIRED OF TALKING.
ALL RIGHT! I'M COMIN' TO GET YA.

BUT AS HE FLEW IN, HIS SNOUT PICKED UP AN ODOR.
OH!
SNIFF
OOF!

OH! GAH! WHAT IS THAT?

IT WAS BACON.
UH-OH.
MAY HURL!
HERE COMES LUNCH!

'CAUSE, YOU KNOW... BACON IS MADE FROM...
LEG
HAM
LOIN
BUTT
RIBS
SHOULDER
NECK
BACON
HOCK
I HAVE TATTOOS!
ACTUALLY, LET'S NOT GO TOO DEEP ON THAT, 'CAUSE IT'S KIND OF AN ICKY AREA.

LET'S JUST SAY BATPIG AND BACON DON'T MIX.

THAT SMELL!

MY POWERS ARE FADING!

FEEL SICK!

THIS IS WORSE THAN THE "MARSHMALLOW PEEPS TILT-A-WHIRL INCIDENT"!

SERIOUSLY, THIS PART IS JUST GROSS. CAN WE GO ON TO THE NEXT CHAPTER?

CHAPTER FOUR

"GIDDY-UP"

MEANWHILE...
SERIOUSLY, MERVIN! NO MORE!
QUIET!! FISH-HORSIES DON'T TALK!

BROOKLYN!!
I'M ON MY LAST FLIPPERS HERE!

BUT BROOK HAD OTHER WORRIES.
CALM DOWN! I THINK GARY'S IN TROUBLE!

OH! GARY!! ARE YOU OKAY?

ARE YOU HURT? I WAS SO WORRIED!

JEEZ. IT WAS JUST A TELEGRAM.

SO, GARY AND BROOK WENT OFF TO DISCUSS STRATEGY WHILE MERVIN ROLLED CARL UP IN A PLACE MAT.

SO. YOU AND BACON, HUH?

OH, YEAH. BARF CITY.

LOOK! LOOK AT THE WINDOW! YOU SEE HER TOO, RIGHT?

SOMEONE HAD FOLLOWED GARY HOME*
QUIET EVIL LAUGH.
*IN A GIANT VILLAIN HOT-AIR BALLOON SHAPED LIKE A BAKED HAM.

How am I GONNa Get IN THat FACTORY, BROOK??
MaYBe We attack BACK?
IS THeRe a SmeLL moRe POWeRFUL THaN BacON IS TO YOU?
ROTTeN FiSH!!
CaRL! We NeeD TO BORROW YOUR USeD GYM SHORtS!

BUT CARL AND MERVIN WERE GONE.
BATPIG

LOOK! THERE'S A NOTE! WHAT DOES IT SAY?

GARY'S HOOVES SHOOK AS HE OPENED THE TINY ENVELOPE.

RIDICULOUSLY LOUD GULPS

CHAPTER FIVE

"UP, UP AND AWAY"

SOMEWHERE, HIGH ABOVE THE CITY...
IT'S A BEAUTIFUL AFTERNOON. ISN'T IT, FISH?
MMMPH MMPH MM MMPHH MMMPH
OH! HA HA! I FORGOT ABOUT THE DUCT TAPE!
BETTER?
WILL PEOPLE STOP DUCT-TAPING MY MOUTH?? THAT'S TWICE IN ONE STUPID BOOK!

WHERE ARE YOU TAKING US??
MERVIN! ARE YOU OKAY??
WHAT'S YOUR EVIL PLAN, BUTCHER?
IS THERE A BATHROOM ON THIS FLYING HAM!?
BACK TO THE FACTORY.
HE'S FINE.
WORLD DOMINATION.
AND, NO. HOLD IT.

WHY DO YOU NEED TWO MILLION DOLLARS?
BUILDING AN EVIL VILLAIN LAIR IS EXPENSIVE.
WHY THE REESE'S CUPS?
THEY'RE DELICIOUS.
WHY A MINIVAN?
FOR HAULING GROCERIES AND STUFF.
AND WHY DO YOU NEED BATPIG'S TRUE IDENTITY?

Because I've Harnessed the Power of Meats and that awful pig goes against everything I stand for and imagine how much meat power can be had from one single Batpig chop??
Oh, so you're just a whack-a-doodle.
NOD NOD NOD

AS THEY UNLOADED ON THE ROOF OF THE FACTORY, THE BUTCHER EXPLAINED.
I ALWAYS THOUGHT IT MIGHT BE GARY, BUT NOW I KNOW FOR SURE.
MMPH.
AND NOW THAT I HAVE YOU GUYS, I'LL...
HANG ON.
UNWRAP
UNWRAP
CRINKLE
CHEW
CHEW
SORRY. QUICK REESE'S CUP BREAK. I'D OFFER YOU ONE, BUT I'M EVIL.

So Gary'll surrender to save you both, I'll destroy him and absorb his meat power and take over the world and there'll be nobody that can stop me.
Questions?
Yes. Where's the bathroom?
mmph!

CHAPTER SIX

"AAAAA!!"

MY PARENTS ARE GONNA KILL ME!
WITH GOOD REASON!!

THEY'LL BE BACK IN AN HOUR! I'VE GOTTA GET MERVIN!!

I DON'T HAVE A CHOICE! I'VE GOTTA GET BACK TO THE BISCUIT FACTORY!
STUPID TIGHT TIGHTS.
BUT HOW WILL YOU GET PAST THE BACON SMELL WITHOUT CARL'S GYM SHORTS?
HOP
HOP

IF ONLY THERE WAS SOME WAY TO BLOCK YOUR ENORMOUS SNOUT!
WOW. ENORMOUS? REALLY? I MEAN, I GUESS IT'S...
WAIT!!
MY EXPERIMENT!
WHAT EXPERIMENT?
COME ON! I'LL SHOW YOU!

AND THERE, IN HIS CLOSET...
TWO CASES OF LIGHTLY EXPIRED SPEARMINT-PUMPKIN GUM!

GARY. WHY DO YOU HAVE ALL THAT GUM?
WELL...
IT BEGAN A FEW DAYS AGO.
NO RESPECT...
I WAS GONNA EXPERIMENT WITH IT TO MAKE A NON-STICKY CHEWING GUM.
END THE FEAR OF STEPPING IN IT FOREVER!
MR. KIM AT THE BODEGA SOLD ME ALL THIS FOR FIFTY CENTS.

BUT... WHAT ARE WE GONNA DO WITH IT?
CHEW IT! AND THEN JAM IT UP MY SNOOTER!
IF I CAN'T SMELL, I CAN'T SMELL THE BACON!
AND I HAVE SUPER SMELLING POWERS (SORRY-I FORGOT TO MENTION THAT), SO WE NEED TO CRAM A TON UP THERE.
LET'S GET CHEWING!

SO THEY CHEWED.
CHOMP CHOMP
CHEW CHOMP
AND CHEWED.
WOW. THIS FLAVOR IS GROSS.
YEAH. (CHOMP CHOMP) IT'S NOT GOOD.
AND CHEWED SOME MORE.
JAW CRAMP!
WORK THROUGH THE PAIN!

DON'T TRY THIS AT HOME. DUH.

CHAPTER SEVEN

"FISH BISCUIT"

ARRIVING BACK AT THE BISCUIT FACTORY, BATPIG SURVEYED THE SITUATION.

NO SIGN OF THE BUTCHER OR MERVIN AND CARL.

YUMMY

JUST THOSE AWFUL BACON PANS AND THE HAM BALLOON.

BUT, LET'S NOT FORGET ABOUT THOSE PIG POWERS. OR PIG-BAT POWERS OR WHATEVER...
ALL RIGHT, X-RAY VISION. DO YOUR THING.
LOOK LOOK LOOK

WHAT HE SAW INSIDE SET HIS HEART TO PUMPING FASTER.
GASP!
X-RAY
X-RAY
MUAH HA HA!
MMPH! MMPH!
THE BUTCHER HAD USED THE BISCUIT DOUGH TO MAKE PIGS-IN-BLANKETS!
NOW TO PREPARE A NICE, TANGY HONEY MUSTARD DIPPING SAUCE.
IT'S GONNA BE OKAY, MERV.
MMPH! MMPH! MMF!
OR, LIKE, ONE PIG AND ONE FISH-IN-A-BLANKET.

IT WAS A BUNCH OF GUYS DRESSED UP AS PORK CHOPS, PLAYING CARDS AND STUFF.

SO, WHEN DO WE DO HER EVIL BIDDING?

WE JUST WAIT FOR THE SIGNAL.

IS YOUR OUTFIT KINDA TIGHT IN THE BUTT TOO?

BATPIG WAS SHOCKED.
WOW! SHE HAS HER OWN ARMY OF BAD GUYS!
I MEAN, DANG!
I THOUGHT SHE JUST THREW THIS TOGETHER, BUT THIS IS, LIKE, A WHOLE THING!
IT'S KIND OF IMPRESSIVE IN A WEIRD WAY.

BUT TIME WAS SHORT, SO HE WENT AHEAD AND SMASHED THROUGH THE WALL.
UNHAND MY FRIENDS, BUTCHER!

AWW. SERIOUSLY? I SPILLED MY HONEY MUSTARD!

YOU HAVE BIGGER PROBLEMS NOW. I KNOW ABOUT YOUR PORKCHOP GUYS.

YOU MEAN MY MINIONS?
WHAT? NO. MINIONS ARE THOSE LITTLE YELLOW GUYS WITH GOGGLES AND–
NO, NO. THE WORD "MINION" WAS AROUND LONG BEFORE THAT.
OKAY. FINE. I JUST DON'T WANT ANY ISSUE WITH DREAMWORKS OR...
THEY'RE MINIONS! MY MINIONS!!

WAIT. WAS THAT THE SIGNAL? I THOUGHT I HEARD "MY MINIONS."
I DIDN'T HEAR IT, BUT I WAS EATING A LOUD CHIP.

REALLY? I MEAN, SHOULD WE CHECK?

DUDE, YOU'RE ALWAYS HEARING THINGS.
JUST PLAY YOUR CARD, SLOWPOKE.

I SAID...
MY MINIONS!!

MAN, THAT'S ANNOYING.

I'M PAYING THESE GUYS TOP DOLLAR.
IT'S SO HARD TO GET GOOD HENCHMEN THESE DAYS...

ENOUGH!

YOUR REIGN OF TERROR IS OVER!

M'KAY. I SEE HOW YOU'D THINK THAT, BUT I HAVEN'T GIVEN MY "BIG EVIL PLAN" SPEECH.

AND YOU HAVEN'T FALLEN FOR THE HORRIBLE SURPRISE.

B

WHAT HORRIBLE SURPRISE ARE YOU TALKING AB—?

YUM YUM!
AAAA!
I THOUGHT YOU WERE A BIG OVEN!

HE iS! BUT He'S SO MUCH MORE!

Meet MY all-iN-ONe "PiG-iN-a-BLaNKeT-MaKiNG ROBOT DOUGH-DiSPeNSiNG OVeN"!!
HaHAHAHa!

I call Him "BLaNKey" FOR SHORT.
B

YES!! BETWEEN MY BUTCHER SKILLS, BLANKEY'S TASTY-TREAT-MAKING SKILLS, AND MY MINIONS, I'LL HARNESS ALL OF THE WORLD'S MEAT POWER! ALL OF IT!!!

YUM YUM! OVEN SET TO 350! TIMER ON!

NOOO!!

YeSSS!

STUFF STUFF

OH, DeaR. BaTPiG SeeMS TO Be IN ReaL TROUBLe.

SERIOUSLY. I THINK I HEARD IT AGAIN!
WHATEVER.
STALLING ISN'T GONNA HELP YOU WIN, BRO.

CHAPTER EIGHT

"SECRET WEAPON"

BROOK HAD (ONCE AGAIN) CONQUERED HER FEAR OF HEIGHTS AND FOLLOWED GARY.

WHILE NO ONE WAS LOOKING, SHE SNUCK IN THROUGH THE BIG HOLE BATPIG HAD LEFT.

SHE HAD A PLAN.

POPPING UP, SHE SIGNALED TO CARL TO BE QUIET.

TIMER ON!

NOOOO!

MMPH!

YESSS!

THEN WHISPERED TO MERVIN.
WHEN I PULL THIS DUCT TAPE, YOU'RE GONNA DO WHAT YOU DO. BUT LOUD, OKAY?

RIIIIIPPP

HEY, LADY! YA BIG WEIRD LADY AND YOUR JANKY-LOOKING ROBOT! YOU THINK YOU CAN SHUT ME UP, YA BIG DUMPSTER-HEAD?!?

THE WHINING ECHOED IN THE FACTORY AND STUNNED THE BUTCHER AND HER ROBOT.

WHA?
YES!
WHA?
BATPIG TUMBLED OUT OF THE OVEN!

MERVIN KEPT IT UP, DRIVING THE ROBOT OUT OF ITS ROBOT MIND.

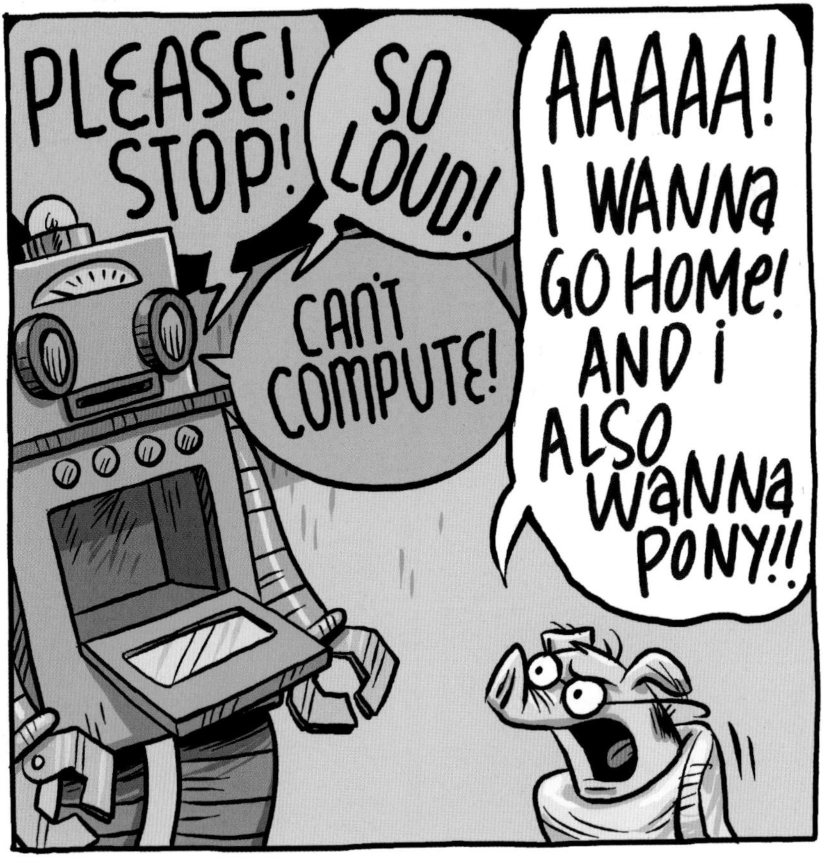

PLEASE! STOP!
SO LOUD!
CAN'T COMPUTE!
AAAAA! I WANNA GO HOME! AND I ALSO WANNA PONY!!

FINALLY, THE ROBOT COULDN'T TAKE IT AND BOUNDED OUT OF THE HOLE IN THE WALL.
I'M OUTTA HERE!
PIGS-IN-A-BLANKET ARE NASTY ANYWAY!!

THE BUTCHER TURNED TO RUN, BUT SLIPPED IN HER SPILLED HONEY MUSTARD.

DARN MY LOVE OF TASTY DIPS!
B

CARL AND BROOK THREW A GIANT WAD OF DOUGH ON TOP OF HER.
HEY!
WOO! HIGH FIVE!

BROOK RAN TO GARY AND FREED HIM FROM HIS "BLANKET."
SOME SUPERPIG I'M TURNING OUT TO BE.
THERE'S NO TIME, GARY! THAT ROBOT IS ON THE LOOSE!
I KNOW. PULL THESE GUM PLUGS. I'M GOING AFTER HIM.

THEN BATPIG FLEW OFF, AFTER THE EVIL ROBOT.
NOSE GUM. EW.
LITTLE HELP?

CHAPTER NINE

"BLANKETS GALORE"

THE ANSWER WAS SURPRISINGLY CLEAR.

SO BATPIG TOOK OFF FOLLOWING THE TRAIL OF THINGS-IN-BLANKETS.
A CAR-IN-A-BLANKET? REALLY?

FINALLY HE TURNED A CORNER AND FOUND THE ROBOT TRYING TO MAKE A NEWSSTAND-IN-A-BLANKET.

STOP!!
YUM YUM!
HEY!

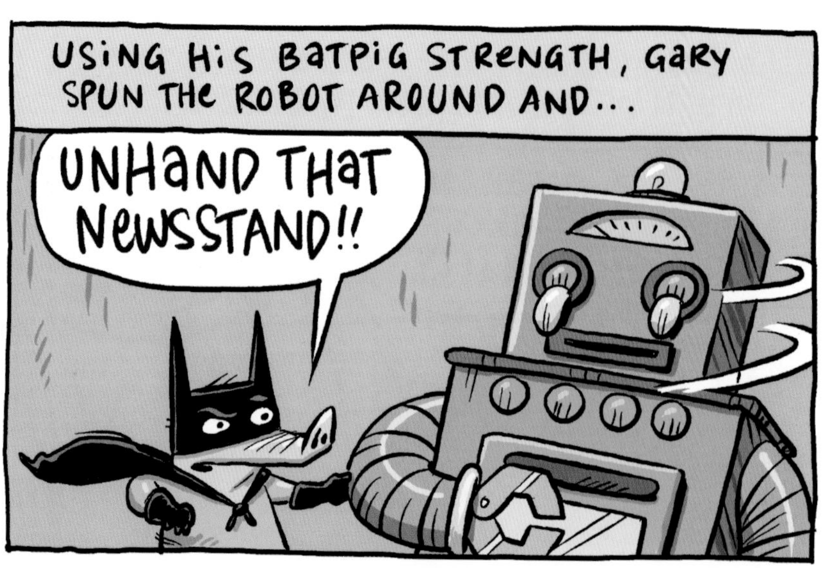

USING HIS BATPIG STRENGTH, GARY SPUN THE ROBOT AROUND AND...
UNHAND THAT NEWSSTAND!!

BUT THE ROBOT APPEARED TO BE CRYING. BIG, GOOEY DOUGH TEARS.

PLEASE STOP ME!

I CAN'T STOP BLANKETING THINGS!

FiNaLLY He SOOTHeD THe ROBOT A BIT WITH His NeW SUPeR-SOOTHING POWeRS. (WHO KNew?) THe TWO SaT DOWN ON THe CURB.

SO, YOU DON'T eNJOY aLL OF THiS?

I MEAN, KINDA. BUT I CAN'T STOP!

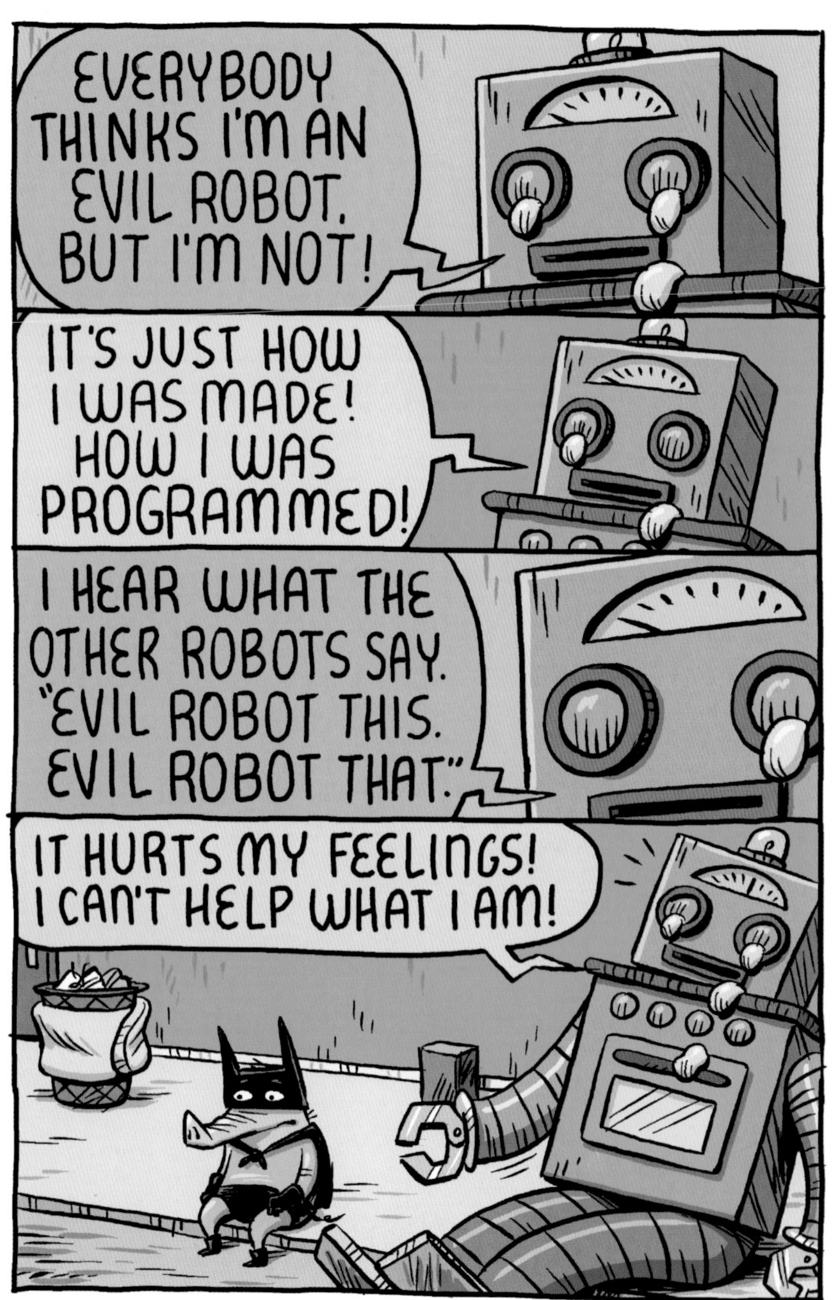
EVERYBODY THINKS I'M AN EVIL ROBOT. BUT I'M NOT!
IT'S JUST HOW I WAS MADE! HOW I WAS PROGRAMMED!
I HEAR WHAT THE OTHER ROBOTS SAY. "EVIL ROBOT THIS. EVIL ROBOT THAT."
IT HURTS MY FEELINGS! I CAN'T HELP WHAT I AM!

GARY THOUGHT ABOUT THAT FOR A BIT.

I UNDERSTAND, BLANKEY.

I REALLY DO.

THERE'S THIS MEAN WOMAN—"THE MEAT LADY"—IN MY NEIGHBORHOOD.

SHE'S ALWAYS MAKING MEAT AND PORK JOKES, JUST LIKE THIS BUTCHER VILLAIN.

BACON JOKES. HAM JOKES.
I CAN'T HELP THAT I'M MADE OF SUPER TASTY MEAT!!

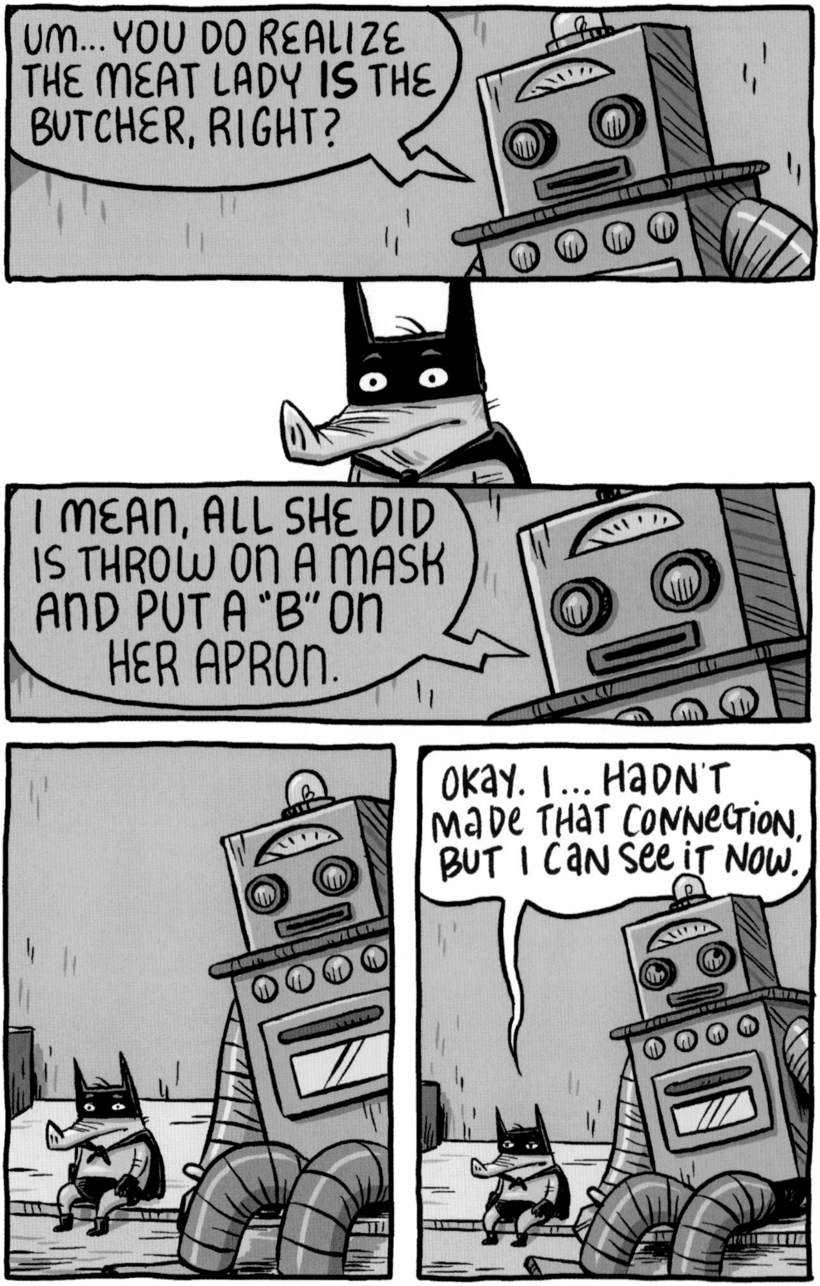

UM... YOU DO REALIZE THE MEAT LADY **IS** THE BUTCHER, RIGHT?

I MEAN, ALL SHE DID IS THROW ON A MASK AND PUT A "B" ON HER APRON.

BUT... I JUST HAD A GREAT IDEA, BLANKEY.

THE TWO TOOK OFF, BATBIG FLOATING BLANKEY ALONG WITH HIS POWERS.
WHEE!

BATPIG LEFT BLANKEY WITH THE GOOD PEOPLE AT THE "VEGETARIAN PIGS-IN-A BLANKETS" FACTORY.
YOU CAN MAKE BLANKETS ALL DAY AND HARM NO ONE!
YAY!
GROOVY, MAN!

MEANWHILE, AT THE BISCUIT FACTORY...
SO, WAIT. GARY IS BATPIG?
I GUESS YOU KNOW NOW, SO YES.
MY COUSIN? GARY??
YES!
BORING, NERDY, DUMB COUSIN GARY?
YES!!
OKAY. I GUESS THAT'S A LITTLE AWESOME.

JUST THEN, GARY FLEW IN.
GUYS! ARE YOU ALL OKAY?
NO, BUT WE'RE NOT DEAD... SO THERE'S THAT.

HE TOLD THEM ABOUT HIS TALK WITH THE ROBOT, AND HIS SOLUTION.

VEGETARIAN PIGS-IN-A-BLANKET SOUND GROSS!
AND YOUR CAPE LOOKS WEIRD!

ALWAYS NICE TO HAVE YOUR INPUT, MERVIN.

BUTCHER AND/OR MEAT LADY, YOU'RE GOING TO JAIL FOR... FOR A...

WAIT. CAN SHE BREATHE UNDER THERE?

I CAN. I CHEWED AN AIR POCKET AROUND MY HEAD.

VERY GOOD. THE POLICE ARE ON THEIR WAY.
NOW THE "MEAT LADY" WILL BE THE "IN-TROUBLE LADY."

KIND OF WEAK. YOU CAN DO BETTER.
HMM.
...LOCK YOU UP. THROW AWAY THE KIELBASA?...
...THROW YOU IN THE SALAMI-ER? INSTEAD OF SLAMMER??
MAYBE YOU JUST SKIP THE "WITTY FINAL WORDS TO THE CRIMINAL" THIS TIME.
YEAH.
IT'S FINE. REALLY. I GET IT.

CHAPTER TEN

"HOME"

TEN MINUTES LATER, GARY AND MERVIN WERE BACK AT THE APARTMENT.
OKAY. WHEW. OUR PARENTS ARE DUE BACK ANY TIME NOW.
WAIT 'TIL I TELL THEM YOU—
NO.
THIS IS OUR SECRET, MERVIN. FOREVER, OKAY?
IF THEY FOUND OUT, I'D BE IN SO MUCH TROUBLE!
SO, THAT'S A BAD THING?

YES, MERVIN. IF I'M GROUNDED FOR ETERNITY, HOW CAN I KEEP THE CITY SAFE FROM EVIL?

FINE.

CAN I BE YOUR SIDEKICK?

NO OFFENSE, BUT I'D RATHER HAVE A BAG OF ROTTEN CANTALOUPES AS MY SIDEKICK.
OKAY... SOLID BURN.

JUST THEN THEY HEARD KEYS IN THE DOOR, AND GARY'S PARENTS CAME IN.

Hi, GUYS. HOW WAS YOUR NIGHT?
BORING.
IT WAS FINE. HOW WAS YOURS?

MY LINGUINE WAS COLD. IT WAS A NIGHTMARE, HONESTLY.

MERVIN STARTED UP AGAIN IN THE HALL.
I WOULD BE THE BESTEST SIDEKICK EVER!
NO. NO, YOU WOULDN'T.
BATBIG AND MERVIN!
NO! BATPIG AND THE MERV-INATOR!!
OKAY. HERE'S MY OFFER.
YOU KEEP THE SECRET... AND DON'T BOTHER ME... AND ONCE IN A WHILE I'LL TAKE YOU OUT FLYING AROUND.
WHAT DO YOU SAY?

OOH. WOW.
I REALLY LIKE BUGGING YOU, BUT...
JUST THEN, GARY'S PHONE STARTED RINGING.
OINK OINK OINK OINK
GASP! THE BATPIG RINGTONE!
BROOKLYN MUST HAVE PROGRAMMED IT WHILE I WASN'T PAYING ATTENTION!
IT'S JUST A DUMB RINGTONE.
SHUSH YOUR FACE! THIS IS AWESOME!
OINK OINK

MY CITY IS CALLING.

OINK OINK

OINK OINK

THE END

THAT'S IT, READERS. UNTIL THE NEXT BOOK. LET'S JUST HOPE BATPIG DOESN'T GO AND GET COCKY OR ANYTHING.

IN THE NEXT BOOK...
BATPIG GETS COCKY!
"SUPER" HERO JUST SEEMS TOO BLAH.
THERE SHOULD BE A BETTER WORD THAN "SUPER".
"SUPER DUPER" HERO, MAYBE?
COMING SOON!!

DON'T MISS ROB HARRELL'S **WINK**, WITH SPECIAL APPEARANCES FROM BATPIG!

TIME Best Book of the Year

Barnes and Noble Children's Book Award Shortlist

NYPL Best Book for Kids

NPR's Book Concierge Pick

Evanston Public Library Great Books for Kids

A Texas Lone Star Reading List Selection

An ALSC Notable Children's Book

"Harrell's genius is making all of it feel authentic for a seventh grader, a teenager who, like countless others, just wants to be normal . . . Bodies change, people change, life continues. It's a lesson a lot of us have been learning, and relearning, in recent days." —*New York Times Book Review*

★ "Filled with the same sardonic humor and celebration of atypical friendships as his Life of Zarf series, [*Wink*] draws from [Harrell's] personal experience to track the wild emotional roller coaster a seventh-grader rides after being diagnosed with a rare tear duct cancer." —*Booklist*, starred review

★ "This page-turner is not to be missed."
—*School Library Connection*, starred review

★ "This lively novel showcases the author's understanding of middle school angst amid the protagonist's experience with a serious illness." —*Publishers Weekly*, starred review

ALSO BY

ROB HARRELL

Life of Zarf: The Trouble with Weasels

Life of Zarf: The Troll Who Cried Wolf

Life of Zarf: Troll Overboard

Monster on the Hill

ROB HARRELL (www.robharrell.com) created the Life of Zarf series, the graphic novel *Monster on the Hill,* and also writes and draws the long-running daily comic strip *Adam@Home,* which appears in more than 140 papers worldwide. He lives with his wife and pup in Indiana.